Madison's "I Didn't Do It!" Hiccum-ups Day

written by Melissa Ryan

illustrated by Ulises Ramos

Madison's "I Didn't Do It!" Hiccum-ups Day

Copyright 2015, estorytime.com

ISBN-13: 978-1522846222

ISBN-10: 1522846220

This book is dedicated to

all the Madison's in the land…sweet
dreams…sleep tight…Love you…
good night.

It was just an average, normal day for Madison as she sat on her front porch with a glass of her favorite milk.

As she raised the glass to her lips, it stopped being a normal day when her chest suddenly jumped and she heard herself make a funny noise.

"HIC!"

It is never a good idea to make sudden moves when you are holding a glass of milk in front of your mouth.

A few moments later, Madison walked into the kitchen with milk dripping down her face, from her hair to her chin.

"Madison, how in the world did you get milk all over your face?" asked Madison's mommy, as she grabbed a paper towel.

"I didn't do it!" Madison said, waving her arms about in the air before she grabbed the towel and sort of wiped the milk off of her face.

"Mommy, I was just sitting down to drink my milk when something hap--"

"HIC!"

The strange thing happened again! Madison was so surprised she jumped and stumbled and grabbed hold of the closest thing to her.

A fruit bowl! Sitting on the edge of the table. And with a squeak of surprise,
Madison fell to the floor and found herself buried by an avalanche of three
apples, four oranges and two bananas!

"It sounds like you have a case of the hiccups," Madison's mommy said with a smile as she dug her daughter out of the pile of fruit and helped her stand up.

"Hiccum-ups? What are hiccum-ups?" Madison asked grumpily. "And how do you stop them?"

Her mommy scooted down to look into Madison's eyes to explain this new sound coming out of her mouth. "Madison, there's no way to get rid of hiccups, you just have to —"

"HIC!"

"—wait for them to go away," her mommy finished. Madison was not happy. She had to put up with these hiccum-ups until they decided to go back to their house? Then they would leave her alone? She shook her head.

No way, she'd find a way to get rid of them herself! She stood straight up, practicing like she was holding her favorite Madison book on her head, and said quite loudly (to her mommy and the fruit bowl)…

"I, Madison, will WIN-- HIC! -- over these silly hiccum-ups!" and she ran out of the kitchen.

"HIC!"

    Pause.

        "HIC!"

There was a small "Thud!" And then silence from the hallway.

"Madison?" her mommy called, "Did you fall down?"

"No!" Madison called back very quickly, followed by the sound of someone quickly getting back on her feet.

And so began Madison's grand adventure to win over her hiccum-ups. Her sister Katherine told her that being scared was the best way to get rid of them. So Madison set about trying to scare herself. But as it turned out, it is very difficult to do that, because you always know you're coming.

Next, Madison tried walking past a mirror and suddenly shouting "BOO!" at herself. Sadly, her mirror self wasn't shocked by this at all and just stared back at her. Then she hiccupped and ended up banging her head on the mirror. "Ouch!"

"HIC!"

Madison sat on her bed with her arms crossed, thinking hard on what to try next. Madison's brother Max walked by and told her Katherine was wrong. Instead, she needed to drink from the far side of a glass to cure her hiccups.

Madison didn't like this idea too much. After all, it was only a little while ago that her hiccum-ups dumped milk all over her face!

"HIC!"

Madison fell off the bed. And so she decided to try the glass trick.

She went to the bathroom and got her special cup with pink ponies on it. Max followed her in case she needed help. She didn't.

She turned on the C-O-L-D water from the sink, filled her cup, when--

"HIC!"

Madison toppled backwards and her cup of water splashed all over Max.
"I didn't do it!" said Madison. "The hiccum-ups did!"

Madison decided to go outside. Nothing inside her house was helping her win her battle over the hiccum-ups. She sat quietly on her swing in her back yard.

She had tried everything, from saying "Boo!" in the mirror, to trying to do a water-in-a-cup trick, to bouncing on her bed as high as she could, to asking her mommy to rub her back. Nothing worked. "I didn't do it!" thought Madison. "I didn't get rid of my hiccum-ups and I really really tried."

Still, it was a very lovely day Madison thought, sitting on her swing. The sun was shining and there was a nice breeze blowing on her face and making her hair dance.

"I suppose--HIC! -- hiccups aren't so bad," Madison said to herself. Then she grinned! She said the word right! Hiccups!

Madison kept swinging as she watched her mother water the flowers outside in the flower pots. She'd been a bit scared when the hiccups started; her insides jumped and jiggled and she worked so hard to try to get rid of them. Madison wasn't scared anymore. She felt them kind of tickle her throat and nose now.

They didn't bother her …they were just silly hiccups that made a funny noise in her mouth. As she was thinking all of these thoughts, Madison realized her hiccups had stopped!

"I did it!" yelled Madison to her mother. "I'm a big girl! I stopped my hiccups!" And she ran to give her mommy a big huge hug and help her water the flowers.

Did you like this book?

I really get excited and encouraged by positive reviews of this book and would appreciate your taking 30 seconds out of your day to give it a review on Madison's book page. Be sure to let your friends know about the estorytime book series. Thank you!

About the Author
Melissa Ryan

is a Mom of five kids, and we all enjoy a love of reading. From my family to yours, and to sweet Madison… enjoy.

Other estorytime books by Melissa Ryan

- ❖ **Madison's "I Didn't Do It!" Hiccum-ups Day**
- ❖ **Good Night Madison and the Moon, It's Almost Bedtime**

These estorytime personalized books are also available in the following personalized first names: Blossom, Sophia, Isabella, Olivia, Rachel, Katherine, Abigail, Mackenna, Mia, Lauren, Barbara, Chloe, Ella, Madison, Addison, Aubrey, Lily, Ava, Sofia, Beth, Zoey, Sheridan, Laurel, Amelia, and Evelyn.

- ❖ **Sleep Tight, Ethan and Sugar Bear, Sleep Tight!**
- ❖ **Carter's Magical Birthday**
- ❖ **Liam's First Train Book**

These estorytime personalized books are also available in the following personalized first names: Jacob, Mason, Ethan, Noah, William, Liam, Jayden, Michael, Alexander, Aiden, Daniel, Matthew, Elijah, James, Anthony, Benjamin, Joshua, Andrew, David, Joseph, Jett, Jackson, and Logan.

Don't see your child's name? Add it! Simply contact estorytime at http://estorytime.com or email info@estorytime.com with your child's name. We'll publish it and contact you to let you know it's ready for your special child.

Order this personalized book as an ebook!

All kids love reading, and nothing says "You're special!" more than a delightful personalized storybook for your child. Now, order it in ebook format too!

Personalized storybooks make wonderful unique gifts for kids of all ages to celebrate new births, birthdays, or any event in your child, grandchild, or favorite child's life.

Watch her imagination blossom, open his eyes in wonderment, and experience the thrill of being a kid...with learning tossed in for fun!

If you don't see her name, no worries – simply go to our website and send us an email requesting the title of the book and your child's name. We will email you when it's ready to download for your Kindle or published in print! Simple! Fast turnaround times.

To order your personalized estorybook, visit: http://estorytime.com

Storytime continues . . .

Follow the adventures of Madison at: **estorytime.com**

Stay in touch with the author via: **melissa@estorytime.com**

Don't Forget! Personalization Available!

If you would like to order this estorybook personalized in another child's name, simply let us know your child's name and we'll let you know when it's published!

1-2-3! Easy way to order:

Email **info@estorytime.com** with book title, your child's name and correct spelling, and if you would like a printed book or ebook or both. We will publish your child's storybook and email you when it's ready to purchase by sending a link to your child's very own online book page. You simply add to your shopping cart, and this is an ideal way to get free shipping if you are a Prime member for printed books. All ebooks are automatic downloads from the Kindle Store. 1, 2, 3 Simple!

Made in the USA
Coppell, TX
31 March 2020